Ladybird books are widely available, but in case of
difficulty may be ordered by post or telephone from:

Ladybird Books – Cash Sales Department
Littlegate Road Paignton Devon TQ3 3BE
Telephone 0803 554761

A catalogue record for this book is available
from the British Library

Published by Ladybird Books Ltd Loughborough Leicestershire UK
Ladybird Books Inc Auburn Maine 04210 USA

© Text and illustrations DC THOMSON & CO LTD 1993
© In presentation LADYBIRD BOOKS LTD 1993

LADYBIRD and the device of a Ladybird are trademarks of Ladybird Books Ltd

The BEANO is a trademark of DC Thomson & Co Ltd

*All rights reserved. No part of this publication may be reproduced,
stored in a retrieval system, or transmitted in any form or by any
means, electronic, mechanical, photocopying, recording or otherwise,
without the prior consent of the copyright owners.*

Printed in EC

DENNIS
THE MENACE

A SACKFUL OF TROUBLE

Ladybird

"Leave it to me! Dad," shouted Dennis, as he raced up the stairs with his faithful hound Gnasher at his heels. "You sit down. I'll collect Mum's breakfast tray."

Dad sat down with a bump! The shock was too much for him. Dennis had just offered to help! It wasn't possible, was it?

Next moment, there was a loud knocking on the front door and a cry of, "Post!". Dad opened the door and was swept off his feet by an avalanche of letters.

"W-what's happening?" cried Dad. "Why have I got all this post?"

"I can guess," said the postman. "They'll all be letters of complaint about your son Dennis... like this one, from me!"

"Oh no," said Dad in a weak voice.

"OH YES!" returned the postman. "Next time Dennis decides to have a sack race he is NOT to use any of my sacks... especially when they're full!"

"Trouble, trouble, trouble," Dad muttered to himself, as he started to arrange the post into a neat pile in the hallway. Before he could finish, Dennis came zooming down the stairs.

"WAHEY!" cried Dennis. "Mum's breakfast tray makes a smashing sledge. HEY, DAD, LOOK OUT!"

But it was too late! CRASH! There was a flurry of things sent flying and Dennis, dog and Dad ended in a mighty mess of mail, milk and marmalade!

"Lucky you were there, Dad, to help me stop," said Dennis, although the expression of anger and purple colouring of his father's face told him that it might not be so lucky after all. "I'll just go and…"

Dad made a noise like an erupting volcano. "So that's why you went for the tray!!! I should have known!"

Dennis was grabbed by the scruff of the neck and placed on top of the mountain of mail.

"Now we'll see what some of these letters have to say about your menacing."

Dad took a letter from the pile. "It seems that Clotsworth's Cream Cake Company invited your school to tour their factory."

"That's right!" agreed Dennis. "They did."

"Yes, but they didn't really expect you to turn up on a pogo stick! You managed to cover everyone in cream by the time you'd finished!"

Dad picked up another letter and groaned. "Dennis, why did you have a peashooter fight outside the kitchens of the Posh Nosh Restaurant?"

"It wasn't my fault the windows were open," protested Dennis. "Anyway, what's wrong with green pea custard?"

"Farmer Brown is – er, was – a good friend of mine," said Dad, looking at another letter.

"I was only trying to help," insisted Dennis. "Farmer Brown's scarecrow wasn't scaring the birds away and his crops were being eaten. So, I tried out MY idea, and it worked, too! I scared the birds."

"Yes, but you also scared EVERYONE else who was passing. Most people don't expect to see a scarecrow suddenly come to life!"

"Beanotown Harriers have written in to say how upset they were that you spoiled their race," went on Dad.

"Aw, but, Dad – I only moved their race direction sign so they could cool down a bit. All that running was making them hot, and a splash in the river was what they needed," said Dennis.

"I dread to think what's coming next," moaned Dad. He picked up a pink scented note tied with a ribbon.

"That's got to be from Walter," murmured Dennis under his breath.

"This is from that nice boy Walter next door," said Dad. "He tells me that he was trying to restuff his teddy when you came along…"

"…and finished the job for him," said Dennis.

"Was it wise to use bone-shaped doggy chocs?" growled Dad. "Gnasher and the rest of the dogs in the neighbourhood chased the poor boy for miles!"

Dennis looked at the huge pile of letters and realised that Dad could go on for hours. He moved his hands and found that the spilt milk had turned some of the paper into a sticky pulp.

Dad shook his head in despair. "All you can do is be a Menace! Why don't you model yourself on Walter and take up a nice, quiet hobby? Dennis, are you listening?"

"Model!" Dennis repeated, staring at the mushy mess that was still on his fingers. He jumped up quickly. "THAT'S IT! GREAT IDEA, DAD! I'll take up model making. I'll start at once!"

Dad was so amazed that he tumbled off the pile of letters he was sitting on.

"Model making? You? Off you go, then!"

Dennis hurried into the garden shed and returned with the hose.

"What are you doing?" asked Dad, looking suspiciously at the hose.

"It's for my new hobby," explained Dennis. "You'll see in a minute!"

Before Dad could say anything else, Gnasher turned on the kitchen tap and a jet of water drenched the mail mountain.

Dennis took great care to see that every one of the letters received a thorough soaking!

At last the hose was turned off. Dad and Dennis surveyed the soft and gooey gunge that covered the hall floor.

"There!" said Dennis, triumphantly. "This will make great papier-mâché for my model making."

"B-b-but..." began Dad, realising that all the letters of complaint had been destroyed.

"Don't worry," continued Dennis, cheerfully, "I'll clear everything away – I'm going to work in the garden." Armed with ladder, pots of red and black paint and the paper sludge, Dennis was soon busily occupied in the front garden.

And here it is – the model that Dennis made – isn't it a beauty?

Dad didn't think so.

"What a monstrosity! New hobby indeed! I might have known that you'd have some trick up your sleeve!"

"Har-har!" chuckled Dennis. "You should know I've only got one hobby – MENACING!"